THE RANCHER'S SECRET BRIDE

HISTORICAL WESTERN ROMANCE

THE BACHELOR'S OF MOONBEAM RANCH
BOOK SIX

TERRI GRACE

PUREREAD.COM

Copyright © 2025 PureRead Ltd

www.pureread.com

All rights reserved. No part of this publication may be reproduced, distributed or transmitted in any form or by any means, without prior written permission.

Publisher's Note: This is a work of fiction. Names, characters, places, and incidents are a product of the author's imagination. Locales and public names are sometimes used for atmospheric purposes. Any resemblance to actual people, living or dead, or to businesses, companies, events, institutions, or locales is completely coincidental.

CONTENTS

Dear reader, get ready for another great story...	1
Prologue	3
1. Father's Wish	11
2. Bitter Memories	20
3. Sweet Reunion	31
4. Joint Effort	37
5. His Missing Family	50
6. Family Is Everything	57
7. New Sisters	65
8. In His Arms	73
9. A Christmas Delight	81
10. Grand Finale	87
Other Books In This Series	95
Our Gift To You	97

DEAR READER, GET READY FOR
ANOTHER GREAT STORY...

A CHRISTIAN WESTERN ROMANCE

Turn the page and let's begin

PROLOGUE

"Promise me that you'll do as I've instructed you, Harvey. Make me that promise so that my heart can find peace." Mr. Benjamin Chester looked at his eldest son, the one who was his pride and joy. They were seated on the brow of the hill overlooking the vast ranch he'd inherited from his father and built up to what it was right now. Moonbeam Ranch reared the best sheep in Montana, and the demand for wool and mutton was high. Benjamin's greatest desire was to leave a befitting legacy for his sons and their generations after them.

"*A good man leaveth an inheritance to his children's children*," Mr. Chester murmured the twenty-second verse from Proverbs chapter thirteen to himself. That was the adage by which he lived, and over the years, it had spurred him to work very hard. His generations after him would arise and call him blessed, for he'd prepared the way for their prosperity. It broke Mr. Chester's heart to see children suffering because their parents didn't work to provide for their futures. He'd purposed from when he'd held his first child in his arms that such a tragedy would never be the portion of his children and their generations after them.

He knew that the kind of burden he was laying on his firstborn son was heavy, but he had faith that his eldest child wouldn't let him down. Harvey was the kind of son every father prayed and hoped for. Not only was he hardworking, but he was kind and treated everyone with respect. Furthermore, as the eldest of five boys, Harvey knew how to keep all his younger brothers in check. His brothers, Jesse, George, Joseph, and Walter, all looked up to him, and that was why his father felt that he could entrust this difficult task to him.

Mr. Chester admitted silently that among his five sons, though he loved them all equally, still there were those who were his favorites. Harvey topped the list of his favorite children, but that was something he would never openly show because the last thing he wanted was to have a divided family. Mr. Chester knew that his wife felt the same way about the boys, too. But not Harvey! He had no favorites among his brothers, and lately they preferred to go to him whenever they needed anything. Jesse, George, Walter, and Joseph all knew that Harvey never took sides. He treated them all equally and fairly.

"Pa, I don't understand," Harvey pulled a piece of grass up from the ground and began to chew on it. He loved these special moments he spent with his father, just the two of them. Lately his father had been bringing him up to this place more and more, and it was early spring, so the weather was fair. They would sit in this spot for hours as they watched over the ranch and whatever was going on down there. From time to time, his brothers would emerge from the house or barns, depending on where they were working, look up and wave, and he would return their greetings. But the four younger boys never once came up here to interrupt this special time Harvey had with his father. Neither did his mother, though she always made sure that she packed sandwiches and enough water for them.

Harvey loved his mother deeply and his brothers too, but his father had his heart, and he would do anything to make him happy.

"Pa, you're talking in riddles as usual."

Mr. Chester laughed, and it ended in a bout of coughing that had him bending over.

"Pa, I'm sorry," Harvey quickly grabbed the canteen at his side, unscrewed the lid and brought it to his father's lips while gently supporting the back of his head. "Drink, Pa. Take small sips and you'll be all right."

When Mr. Chester had caught his breath, he nodded his gratitude to his son. It was time to tell him everything.

"Harvey, the time has come when I can no longer conceal anything from you. You know that I've been ill for a long while, and I've made my peace with all this. My time nears its end, and when I'm gone, I don't want you, your mother, or your brothers to mourn for me for too long. I don't want your Mama and younger brothers to know how ill I am, at least not yet. Strengthen yourself because you'll have to hold the family together. The Lord whom I serve will be with you and guide you in all your ways. I know many fathers leave wealth to their children and expect that they'll be all right. But I leave you more than just material wealth, Harvey. I've brought you up in the ways and admonitions of the Lord, and my prayer is that you'll never depart from them. Let the Lord be your guide always, and this journey won't be too hard. One day when we shall meet again at the feet of our Lord Jesus Christ, He will say to both of us, '*Well done, good and faithful servants.*' Do you understand what I'm saying to you?"

Harvey nodded even as he fought back his tears. In all his years of growing up, his father had seemed larger than life and indomitable. But in the past few months, Harvey had seen changes in his face. The once-intense gray eyes, which he and his brothers had inherited, were now watery with pain, and he coughed a lot. Harvey had even once seen blood on his Pa's handkerchief after a violent bout of coughing. Yes, he knew that his father was seriously ill, but he didn't want to imagine a time when this wonderful man wouldn't be around.

"Promise me, Harvey," Mr. Chester clasped his son's right hand in both of his and brought it to his heart. "Promise me that you'll keep this family together. My son, promise me that you'll stand by your Mama and raise your brothers in the ways of the Lord and never allow them to turn to the world and all its temptations. Harvey, promise me that when the time comes, you'll make sure that your brothers, and of course yourself, will find godly and virtuous women to marry. Son, if you marry the wrong woman, then your life will be full of pain and misery. Marriage must never be taken lightly. God Almighty ordained marriage, and He wants His children to have little heavens here on earth and raise up a godly generation. Godly families make a strong society and nation, and the opposite is also true. Now promise me that all the things I've asked of you, you'll do."

"Pa," Harvey swallowed painfully. "I promise you."

"And another thing, your mother is still young and very beautiful. When I'm gone, she may find love again. Be the rock of the family and watch over your brothers should your mother decide to remarry and go to live with her new husband. Don't oppose her even if you feel that she should stay with you. Let her live her life because she's a good woman, and for these fifteen years or so, we've had a wonderful marriage and life together. I just wish that I had more time to be with my lovely wife, Josephine, and you, my sons."

"Pa, I thought the doctor said that you were getting better."

Mr. Chester smiled sadly, "I thought so too, but I have to face reality and accept what is to come. But I leave my blessings with you, my son." The middle-aged man placed his right hand on his son's head and raised the left one high. "God of my father whom I serve, this is Your servant Benjamin before You with my son, my firstborn, Harvey. Lord, my time to leave this earth draws nigh, and I pray that Your blessings, protection, and favor will be upon Harvey as he represents his brothers. Give him wisdom, knowledge and understanding, for he's yet a small boy and can't do it on his own. Lord, be his guide always."

FATHER'S WISH

Fifteen Years Later

Four weddings in the family in the space of just eight months was quite an achievement. Harvey smiled as he stood on the portico and watched his four brothers and their wives laughing under the quaking poplar tree planted by their grandfather many years ago when he first acquired this land.

There was so much laughter and happiness on the ranch because of his four new sisters-by-marriage, and Harvey wondered how they'd survived without these lovely women. And the laughter of children was also heard on the ranch once again and it warmed Harvey's heart. This is what his father wanted, and more than ever, Harvey wished he were still alive to see his dreams of a growing family come to pass.

His sister-in-law, Glenda, who was Joe's wife, had her twin sisters living with them. The girls were about four years old now, and since their arrival nearly six months ago, had become the life and pulse of the homestead. Everyone loved them, and it wasn't strange to find his burly cowboys carrying them around or even riding with them. Harvey enjoyed spending time with the girls, who were so innocent and inquisitive. They made him think deeply, yet seeing the twins running around the compound very happily and freely also brought tears to Harvey's eyes.

It was late autumn, but the weather was still warm and that's why the family members were able to sit under the poplar tree and have a wonderful time together. There was a slight breeze, which was manageable as the sun still shone.

Alicia and Alison, Glenda's twin sisters, ran up to him, their puppy Rusty hard on their heels.

"Uncle Harvey, what are you doing?" Alicia held onto his leg and looked up at him, an adorable smile on her face. Harvey's breath caught in his throat as he thought about some other twins somewhere else.

Where were his own children, and how were they coping without their father being in their lives? Seven years ago, his lovely wife Sally had left home, and it was all because of his mother. And you, too, a small voice added, fueling the guilt that seemed to be his constant companion.

Throughout their brief marriage, he'd had to put up with constant complaints from his wife about his mother. He'd just thought it was women's normal spates because mothers-in-law and their daughters-in-law were often at loggerheads. Some of his friends told stories of their homes being warzones, and they'd always laugh about it and compare stories.

Now he felt ashamed of how he'd remained silent when he was quite aware that his mother was ill-treating his wife. At some point he'd discovered that their fights weren't normal but bordered on malice on his mother's part. Yet he'd done nothing to protect Sally and his unborn children, and in the end, his wife had been driven out of her matrimonial home. Harvey suspected that his mother had something to do with Sally's disappearance, even though she'd vehemently denied any wrongdoing on her part. According to his mother, Sally had only been after his money, and when she was expected to pull her weight around the home, she'd fled.

"*Such a woman was only with you because of what she could gain,*" *Mrs. Chester had told him.* "*Sally thought she would reign as queen in this home, but one can never reap where they've not sowed. I guess the shame of being a worthless person who is trying to take advantage of an innocent man made her leave. Don't worry, Son; there are better girls out there and soon you'll find yourself just the right kind of woman you deserve.*"

Then his mother had died just months later, but he hadn't gone to bring his wife back home because of shame. At the time, he'd been unable to cope with much else because the ranch needed his full attention, as did his four brothers. Suddenly the five of them had become total orphans and his brothers had been badly affected. Struggling to keep the family together, while also ensuring that the ranch's affairs were running smoothly, was too much for him and he'd sunk all his efforts and strength in these endeavors.

He'd kept telling himself that when things eased up at the ranch he would go and bring his family back, but time just flew past. Running an outfit as huge as Moonbeam Ranch was no mean feat, and many times he'd had sleepless nights as he tried to hold everything together. Harvey's greatest fear was failing his father, who'd entrusted the ranch and his brothers to him. Now seven years later, his larger family was doing very well, while the immediate one was still out there in the cold.

Though he'd quickly found Sally after his mother's death, for she'd taken refuge at the church, he still hadn't made any move to bring her back home. At the time he'd told himself that she would return home on her own. But then he heard that she'd left Beaverhead, and that shocked him because he wasn't aware that she had family elsewhere. But he soon found out that it was the pastor who'd found her a position as a schoolteacher at one of the church's schools in Butte.

The thought that she was under the church's supervision had given him some respite, but still he hadn't reached out and tried to bring his wife and children home. Though, with the help of the pastor, Harvey had been able to know how they were faring on. Unknown to Sally, Harvey had been supporting her through her pregnancy, and this went on when she put to bed and brought forth his twin children, Andrew and Andrea. Seven years later, he was still supporting his family in secret.

"Uncle Harvey," he looked down to find that the twins were still with him. "What are you doing?" Alicia asked. "Carry me up to the sky," she raised her hands in the air. 'Up, up." And the two of them ran around him in circles, shouting at the top of their voices, and Harvey laughed even as he winced a little.

"Little girls, you don't give up, do you?" Harvey picked them up one by one and swung them high in the air. Their delighted shrieks filled the air, and for a moment, his heart was comforted.

The twins soon got tired of the game and went back to running around the compound with their puppy. Harvey watched them for a while as his thoughts went back to his family.

Though Harvey had continued to support his wife, he'd asked the pastor to never reveal that secret to her. Sally was highly intelligent, and if the pastor gave her too much money at once, she'd quickly realize that help was coming from elsewhere, not the wages from the school. Then she would begin asking questions, and Harvey was sure that if she found out that he was supporting her and their children, she would reject the aid. Sally was that kind of a person. Not even his mother offering her money had made her change her mind about marrying him. But Harvey was sure something else had forced her out of their home seven years ago.

"Brother, why don't you come and join us," George called out. "Don't just stand there looking so much alone while we're here."

Harvey smiled and waved at his brothers. He couldn't help thinking that his father would have been very proud of the men they'd all become. His eyes went to Jesse, the second born in the family and the one who'd just recently gotten married.

Of all his brothers, Jesse had been the unluckiest when it came to love. Twice, he'd thought he'd found love, but the women all turned out to be nothing but money-hungry women. That was until Charlotte, or Charlie as she was called, came into his life. Charlie was his other sister-in-law's cousin. She'd come to the ranch as their housekeeper and happened to bring her cousin Sophie along. Jesse had found love at last when he opened his heart to Charlie, and now was a very happy man.

Sophie had come at the right time when his third-born brother George was recuperating and had lost hope of ever walking again. He'd been injured as he was training to become a rodeo rider and the local doctor had said that he would never walk again.

But Sophie's care and determination had brought George from the depth of despondency and given him life again. They'd fallen in love and were married just few weeks before Jesse and Charlie.

Then there was Joe, who'd fallen in love with Glenda, a young woman who'd fled from her stepfather's scheming to have her married to his older widowed brother. Glenda had been sent by her dying mother to Beaverhead to find a man who turned out to be her father. Mr. Owen Russell had worked at Moonbeam Ranch for years but had died seven years before Glenda showed up. Just before Glenda came to Moonbeam Ranch, his brother Joe had discovered a terrible secret about their mother.

It turned out that Glenda's father, Mr. Russell, had sent her mother away when she was carrying her in her womb. Mr. Russell had been carrying on a secret, illicit relationship with Harvey's mother for years. His mother was the reason Mr. Russell had sent his wife and unborn child away. That was the secret they'd uncovered just a week or so before Glenda arrived at the ranch with her own letter given to her by her mother on her death bed. Glenda's mother had instructed her to come to the west and deliver a letter to Mr. Owen Russell, but it had come too late. Owen had passed away seven years before.

Glenda had come to Moonbeam Ranch and fallen in love with Joe, and they'd been married for the past four months.

Walter was the one who'd started all this, and Harvey raised his head to look at his youngest brother. Walter had his wife Lauren on his lap and his hand over her slightly swollen abdomen. They'd just shared the wonderful news that they were expecting their first child.

Harvey sighed as he decided to join his siblings and their wives. More children would be born into the family and run around the hallways of this vast house. They would call him uncle and he would play with them, loving them deeply because they were his blood.

Yet his own real blood offspring remained out there in the cold. Perhaps it was time to bring his family home where they belonged.

"You all look like you're enjoying yourselves very much. But mind the weather, and especially the little ones. This fall the weather may seem warm but there's a chill in the air that could cause trouble for you." Harvey was overly protective of his family. He suddenly noticed that the twins and their faithful companion Rusty were missing. Their happy shouting had ceased. "Where are Alicia and Alison?" He asked.

"They went to get some orangeade from the kitchen," Glenda answered. "Ah! Here come the terrors," she smiled at the two girls as they came running straight to Harvey and begged him to once more lift and swing them up in the air.

Harvey obliged the twins while hiding his own pain behind the forced laughter. His own twins were now six years old, and he'd missed out on all the milestones of their growth. He hadn't been there to watch Sally and take care of her during the period she was carrying them in her womb. He hadn't been there when they took their first breath on this earth, nor had he been there for their first little cries. He'd missed their first steps, teething, the words they spoke, and the love children poured out on their father. Sally had the love of their twins, and for all these years, Harvey was envious of the privilege his wife had enjoyed.

"Higher," Alicia screamed, and Harvey did as bid.

"That's quite enough," Glenda rose to her feet. "These two need to eat their lunch and take naps. Come along," she held her hand out for the twins.

Harvey felt sorry that their game had come to an end.

"See you later children," Harvey called out while waving at them. He then sat down beside Joe, feeling like the odd man out.

BITTER MEMORIES

Salome Franklin was walking down the street in a cheerful mood as she thought about her lovely children, when she spotted someone who caused her to quickly duck into a milliner's store in central Butte, her heart pounding hard. When she was out of sight, she breathed a deep sigh of relief. There was no way that he would come into this store and find her.

After seven years of being apart from the man who was still her husband and who she continued to love with her whole heart, seeing Harvey Chester again sent her heart racing. But he was the last person she ever wanted to see again. And he was here in Butte! She was glad that she'd spotted him first, so she was able to hide from him before he'd seen her.

For seven years she'd wondered how she would act when she saw him again. Her lips tightened as she thought about how he'd always brushed aside any complaints she'd made to him about his mother.

"My darling," he would tell her, "Mama loves you but she's very conservative. We just need to give her a little time to get used to our marriage. We got married in secret and she wasn't happy about it. You know that every mother's greatest desire is to plan her children's weddings. Mama feels like we denied her that chance and that's why she's angry. But she'll soon come around, and then you'll be very good friends; you'll see. And maybe on the first anniversary of our wedding we can let her plan some large reception to appease her."

But that had never happened and here they were now—separated for seven years and not once had Harvey come to look for her and their children. It was as if he'd forgotten about them and moved on with his life. So, seeing him across the street a few minutes ago had really unnerved her.

"Miss, are you interested in buying any one of our hats?" A soft voice reminded her of where she was.

"Yes," she said, turning around to smile at the saleslady who looked to be in her early twenties. Sally searched through the simple hats on the different racks for something within her price range. Andrew and Andrea needed hats because she wanted them to take up riding. They were growing very fast, and it seemed as if she was always having to get new clothes for them, including hats and shoes.

But for the church's charity, she might not have been able to cope with raising two children on her own. Pastor Vincent's wife, Melissa, had tried many times to tell her to seek help from her husband. But that was the one thing she'd purposed never to do.

Harvey's mother had called her a greedy leech who wanted to reap where she hadn't sowed. She'd been called a poor beggar who wanted to use Harvey as a ladder to climb up from the pit where she belonged.

The salesgirl once again reminded her where she was, and she quickly purchased two hats for her children and a small feathered one for herself. The amount of money she spent at the store ate into what she'd intended to use for groceries, but she felt that it was worth it. She loved seeing the smiles on her children's faces whenever she bought them new things.

"Mama, you're a good person," Andrew said when she got home and presented the twins with their gifts. "It's not our birthday, but you bought us these lovely hats. Thank you, Mama."

"My love," Sally kissed her son's forehead, then Andrea's, too. "Your Mama doesn't have to wait for your birthdays to buy you gifts. Besides, I'd like for you to learn how to ride, and you'll need these hats to keep the heat from harming you."

"Thank you, Mama," Andrea said. "This hat fits me very well."

"So does mine," and they donned their hats.

As the twins strutted up and down the living room showing off their new hats to her, Sally swallowed painfully. More and more, Andrew was looking like his father; and Andrea, her grandmother. It was very funny how Andrea ended up looking so much like the grandmother who'd rejected her before she was even born.

Sally had come across Mrs. Chester's obituary in one of the weekly magazines soon after the twins were born, and for a moment, she'd felt sorry for the woman. Because of her cruelty and rejection, Mrs. Josephine Chester would never see her grandchildren. She would never see more generations after her, and that was a missed blessing.

Sally had lost her own parents and been brought up by an aunt who'd been opposed to her relationship with Harvey right from the start.

"Sally my dear, their kind can never mix with the likes of us. We're not of their class and social standing. I fear that once you get married to that boy, his family will treat you badly. Be prepared for a lifetime of heartache if you dare to give your heart to that man. Please don't lose your heart to one who is unworthy of you, Sally."

But Sally had turned a deaf ear to her aunt's pleas. She was in love, and Harvey had promised her the sun, the moon, and the stars, all served to her on a golden platter. She'd believed and trusted him, so when he suggested that they get married in secret, she hadn't hesitated at all.

"It's the only way to force my mother's hand," Harvey had told her in very convincing tones. "Once she sees that we're married, there's nothing she can do but accept our union."

But her husband had been wrong, oh how wrong he'd been! The moment Mrs. Chester found out that they were married, she'd nearly brought the roof down.

"Never will I accept such an unsuitable union," Mrs. Chester had screamed. "No one in society will accept a union such as this one. There's nowhere that light can mix with darkness and be one."

"Mother, we're already married, so you just have to accept that Sally is my wife," Harvey had told her. "Besides, you don't control our lives, Ma. I'm no longer a child, and I know what I'm doing. My decision to marry Sally has given me a lot of peace, so I believe that we did the right thing."

"You think so? You call this nonsense doing the right thing?" Mrs. Chester had hissed. "We'll see who's in control."

And for the next few weeks, she'd tormented Sally. For one, she refused to sit at the same table with Sally, and Harvey's brothers were forbidden from as much as even looking her way. They were informed that Sally was one of the maids in the house. The cook and housekeeper would only serve Sally when Harvey was around. Otherwise, she was forced to go hungry, and Sally was in despair. She refused to regret her marriage to Harvey because she believed that he loved her and would fight for her.

But each time she complained about his mother's ill-treatment, he simply brushed her fears aside. And in the end Mrs. Chester had showed them who was in control. When she found out that Sally was expecting a child, things became even worse.

"If you don't leave my home and this town immediately, you won't live to bring forth that child you're carrying. I even wonder if it's really my son's child that you're carrying. I have my doubts, and if you think you have my son fooled, I'm not so gullible."

Those nasty words had cut deep into Sally's soul. She'd come into the marriage as a virtuous woman, and she loved Harvey too much to ever wrong him. Yet his mother had made her feel lower than a heel, and that's what made Sally realize that she would never be accepted into this family.

On the day she'd left Moonbeam, it was Jesse Chester who'd found her walking along the road carrying her bag, and he'd taken her to the pastor's place, for that's where she'd decided to seek refuge.

"Harvey loves you," he'd told her as she wept silently on the seat beside him in the buggy. "Have faith that one day all will be well, and he'll come back for you."

"How did you know it's all about Harvey?"

Jesse smiled, "Mama may think that calling you a servant will hide the truth. I know that you and Harvey are married even if you've been keeping things secret. My brother is a good man and one day soon he'll come to his senses. Harvey's only problem is that he listens to our mother too much, and it's as if her word is the law to him. But don't worry, when I get the chance, I'll speak to Harvey about all this."

"No please, don't talk to him about anything. I'm leaving because I'll never belong with your kind. Just let things be, I'll be all right."

But even though Sally had held onto hope that Harvey would return for her, the day had never come. Even after his mother had died, Harvey hadn't bothered to find her and their children.

He was probably married to a woman of his mother's liking and class, and maybe they even had children. That thought hurt her deeply; that it had been easy for Harvey to forget all about her and her children. Well, he had no idea that she'd given birth to twins.

It was very clear that all the promises he'd made that he would love her forever had been lies. No, Harvey and his kind married their own kind, and not one like her.

Sally wiped her tears and rose to prepare dinner for them as the twins danced around their small living room.

∽

SILENCE IS what Sally dreaded the most, especially when one was dealing with children. And she should know! As a teacher, the only time she welcomed silence was when the students were working on something she'd given them. But when it was time to play and they were all silent, something was going on. Either the children were in trouble or causing it.

She'd been humming to herself as she prepared the twins' favorite lunch of mashed potatoes and thick mutton gravy. Anytime she made their favorite meals, the twins would be all around her asking if they could help in any way. But not today! At first Sally thought they were doing their school homework. Though school was in session for the first semester of the year, Reverend Philip, the new pastor at church, had insisted on shutting down for a couple of weeks because the buildings needed some renovations.

Fall was warm, but the winter promised to be very chilly, and the pastor had expressed concern that the roof over the two-room schoolhouse was loose, and there were cracks on the floor. He'd also talked about tearing down the wall on one side of the schoolhouse and rebuilding it anew.

The students had rejoiced at having two whole weeks of holiday, but Sally and her colleague, Martha Lander, had groaned. Missing two weeks of school meant that they would have to work harder this semester to cover the time lost. But since there was nothing she could do about it, Sally took it all in her stride.

She always gave her children work to do in the mornings when they were bright and chirpy and then used the afternoons for either craft work or if the weather allowed it, taking a hike and a picnic. There was so much to be learned from nature around them, and Sally wanted her children to grow up loving and appreciating nature, for it was the Lord's loving gift to His creatures.

But today something was definitely wrong. "Andrea, Andrew?" She took the food off the stove and walked to the back door of the house. "Where are you? It's not time for hide and seek yet, where are you?" She could see their slates on the small porch at the back of the house, but they were nowhere to be seen. "Lunch is almost ready, and I don't want it getting cold," she called out.

Her next-door neighbor, Mrs. Chase was standing on her own back porch watching her children. "Good afternoon, Rita," she called out. "Have you seen Andrea and Andrew? Are they playing with Mark and Jocelyn?"

"Good afternoon, Sally. No, I haven't seen the twins this morning. Mark and Jocelyn were indoors this whole time, and I only just let them out right now. They could be on the other side of the house."

Sally wasn't worried at first because the twins tended to get caught up in some activity or other and forget time and all else. She decided to check inside the house first just to be sure they weren't taking a nap. Their bedroom was empty, and the beds neatly made. Her bedroom was also neat, a clear indication that they hadn't jumped on her bed like they often did. She noticed that one of the drawers of her bedside stand was standing open but didn't pay much attention to it. She'd probably forgotten to shut it after taking something out.

"Andrew and Andrea," her tone changed when she couldn't find them. They were probably hiding so she would search for them. They loved doing that! "This isn't funny anymore. Come out now so I can serve lunch. If you don't get here at once, you'll go hungry for the rest of the day. And you'll be sparing me the time to prepare dinner this evening."

But the twins were nowhere to be found, and when the

neighbors realized that she was searching for her children, a few came out to help.

By two in the afternoon when she couldn't find her children, Sally nearly broke down. The twins had never wandered far from home, and usually hunger brought them back. No matter where they were or what they were doing, once one of them got hungry, they would come back home.

Her children were missing, and Sally knew fear like never before.

SWEET REUNION

Harvey did a doubletake when he saw the woman standing outside the front door. He'd been reading the newspaper at the dining table as he waited for his afternoon coffee when the knock came. Since the housekeeper was busy on the other side of the house, he rose to get the door. His estranged wife was the last person he expected to find standing at the door.

"Sally?" He thought his eyes were deceiving him. "Sally is this really you?" This was the woman he'd loved so deeply and never stopped thinking about all these years. Then he noticed that she seemed agitated. "What's wrong, love?"

To her consternation, Sally burst into tears and covered her face with her palms. Then she felt strong large arms going around her and resisted only a little. With a sob she allowed herself to be engulfed in the warmth she'd missed so much. Being in her husband's arms nearly made her forget why she was here in the first place, when she'd purposed in her heart years ago that she would never return.

"Please come in," Harvey said softly, leading the still-crying woman into the house.

Sally couldn't believe that she was here in this house again. She'd never thought that she would ever set foot over the threshold of this house again, not after the last time when she'd fled to protect her own and her unborn children's lives.

"Sally, I don't like seeing you like this," Harvey said, helping her to the large couch and sat beside her. Then he brought out a hankie and wiped her tears. "What has happened?"

"I don't know what to do," Sally wrung her hands. "It's the twins."

"Twins?" Harvey feigned ignorance. "What are you talking about?"

Sally looked down and sniffed. "The children," she bit her lower lip nervously. "When I left here seven years ago, I was expecting your child, and they turned out to be twins. A girl and a boy, and I named them Andrea and Andrew. They're six years old now."

Even though Harvey had always known about his children, hearing the words from his wife's lips deeply moved him. She had finally acknowledged that he was the father of their children.

"I have twin children?"

"Yes, but right now I don't know where they are."

Harvey's heart nearly stopped. "What do you mean you don't know where they are?"

Sally wiped her tears, "I was preparing their lunch and then suddenly I realized that the house was too silent. I went to check on them but couldn't find them anywhere. So, I searched everywhere for them but couldn't see them. Our neighbors helped me search, but we couldn't find the twins. My children are missing, and I'm so afraid for them."

Harvey once again took his wife into his arms to comfort her.

"Sally my love, please don't cry. All will be well. We'll find our children, and I believe that wherever they are, God has kept them safe. Nothing will happen to them."

"Oh Harvey," Sally sobbed. "I'm very sorry that I never told you about them before today. Please forgive me."

"I don't hold it against you, my dear wife. Please forgive me for not being there for you when you and our children needed me. Please forgive me for not standing up to my mother and for allowing her to make you leave our home. And because I didn't protect you, now our children are missing. But I promise that I'll do everything in my human ability to find our children. I won't rest until I restore our children into your loving arms."

"Why didn't you come?" Sally's voice was low.

"What did you say?" Harvey released her and looked into her face.

Sally raised tear-filled eyes to him. "You always said that it was your mother who didn't want you to marry me. You said that it was because of Mama that I needed to be patient and one day she would accept me. Yet after she died, you never came to look for us. You never even tried to find us." She moved away from him. "It's clear that your mother was never the problem. You never really loved me and were simply using your mother as an excuse to get rid of me. You made it clear that we belong in different worlds."

"No, no, no," Harvey tried to pull Sally into his arms again, but she resisted him. She rose to her feet and moved to the other side of the living room. She looked around and noticed vast changes, only those made by the hand of a woman.

Sally knew that Mrs. Chester was dead, so clearly there was another woman keeping the house, and not just the housekeeper. There was a difference between homes kept by servants and those which had a mistress of the house.

Sally wasn't aware that any of Harvey's brothers were married but she hadn't seen any of them for seven years. She didn't know anything about them, and that had been deliberate. Everything concerning Harvey was taboo to her, and she'd made sure she didn't think about him, nor try to find out anything to do with his family.

"Seven years, Harvey," Sally said, shaking her head. "Your mother died just a few months after the twins were born. I thought you would have tried to find us, but no, you went on with your good life while I struggled to raise your children all alone."

"Sally please," Harvey could feel her pain. "I never stopped loving you. You're all I thought about all these years, and just so you know, I could never move on even when my mother tried to get me to do so. I love you so much."

"Don't say that to me," Sally hissed at her husband. "Don't lie to me because I'm no longer that naïve nineteen-year-old girl you deceived with all your flowery and flattering words. None of them were true anyway. You made me marry you because I believed that you loved me the same way I loved you. No, Harvey, I didn't just love you; I adored you and would have laid my life down for you, which I did in a way. Yet for you it was just a way of showing your mother that you were in control of your own life. It was never about me at all, and I learned that the hard way."

"Sally," Harvey approached her, holding out his arms.

"Don't come near me," she dashed her tears away. "I don't want to hear any more lies from you. In any case, that's not why I came. My children are missing and that's what's important right now, not bygones that should be put behind us."

"Sally..."

She held her hand up, "If you want to talk to me about our missing children, then so be it. But spare your breath if you want to give me nothing but more lies.

Harvey could see that nothing he said would convince his wife that he still loved her. But she was a hurting mother right now and all that was on her mind was her children. His children!

He was going to do all he could to find their children, so she'd be happy again. Then when she was reconciled with their children, it would be time for him to do all he could to get his wife back. Seven long years of loneliness, pain, frustration, and living in despair must come to an end. No, he would never return to that state of desolation ever again.

He wanted his wife back; he needed to have his children grow up in their home. It was time for him to make strides and bring his family back home where they belong.

JOINT EFFORT

～

Sally slumped back onto the couch and realized how bone weary she was.

"What am I going to do?" She was a bundle of nerves.

"We're in this together, Sally," Harvey said as he handed her a glass of water he'd poured from the jug on the tray on the dining table. "I'm here for you whenever you need me."

Sally gave him a cold look, reminding herself that he'd never been there for her when she'd needed him before. Could she trust him to keep his word? "Were it not because my children are missing, I would never have set foot in this home or this land ever again."

"Sally please," the front door opened, and Harvey turned to see his brothers Jesse and George walking in with their wives.

"What's going on?" Jesse looked from Harvey to Sally. "Sally, is this really you?" He sounded really happy to see her. "Welcome back. I'm so happy to see you again."

Sally smiled at one of her favorite people in the world. "Jesse, it's good to see you too. How have you been?"

Jesse moved closer and hugged Sally. "You've been crying," he held her shoulders then looked at his brother, a slight frown on his face. "Harvey, what have you done to Sally?"

"No, it's not him," Sally laughed, then noticed that the woman who'd come in with Jesse was observing her curiously.

"Sally, this is Charlie, or Charlotte, my wife," he turned to his wife. "Charlie darling, this is Sally. She's Harvey's wife."

"What?" George burst out. "When did Harvey get married?" He looked at his two brothers. "Can someone please tell me what's going on?" He looked hard at Sally. "Years ago, I remember Sally coming to this house and living here for a while, but I always thought she was a servant or something. Harvey's wife you said, huh! Did they just get married today or something? How are we just hearing about this right now?"

Jesse chuckled, "No brother, Sally here and Harvey were married seven years ago."

George stared in disbelief at his brother and Harvey nodded in confirmation. "We have twins, and their names are Andrea and Andrew. They're six years old now."

"I don't believe this," George shook his head. "Are you telling me that Harvey has a family that we didn't know about? Do Joe and Walter know about this?" Jesse shook his head. "This is just astonishing. Harvey and Sally are married?"

"It's true," Harvey said. "Sally is my wife."

"What happened? Whey doesn't your family live with us? Where are the children now? Will Sally live with us again?"

"George, too many questions at a time," Jesse stopped smiling. "There's a long story behind all this, but right now let's just be glad that Sally is back." He turned to her. "Dear sister-in-law, I pray that you're here to stay for good. But wait, where are the twins? I didn't see any children outside."

"That's why Sally is here," Harvey said. "The twins are missing."

"What do you mean missing?" Jesse looked startled.

Harvey sighed, "Sally was preparing lunch for the children at her home earlier this morning when they left the house and have been gone for a long while."

"Sally lives in Beaverhead?" George asked.

"No, I live in Ennis, but I used to live in Butte before that. We lived in Butte for seven years, from the time I left this house, and it's only recently that we moved to Ennis," Sally sniffed. "I moved to Ennis so the children would be closer to their father's home," she half whispered.

Jesse and George looked at each other and Harvey could almost guess what they were thinking. That if his wife and children were this close, how is it that he hadn't brought them home yet?

"We need to go out and find my children," Harvey said. There would be time enough for explanations and recriminations later. Right now, he needed to find his children before darkness descended on the land. "Where are Walter and Joe at this time?"

"They should be here any moment now, seeing as they were right behind us," Jesse said, and then they heard footsteps out on the portico. "Aha! That must be them now."

And sure enough, Joe and Walter walked into the house and Harvey repeated what he'd just shared with Jesse and George.

"Were the twins in the habit of going to people's houses to play?" Harvey asked.

"No. My children wouldn't go to anyone's home without first letting me know about it. In any case, none of the neighbors saw them today, and we looked everywhere for them. I've taught Andrea and Andrew all about the dangers of leaving home without my permission and they would never do it," Sally started crying softly. "Where are my children, what's happening to them now? They must be really scared. My children have never been disobedient to me, why did they leave home like that? Or did someone entice and kidnap them from home?"

"No, don't say that!" Harvey nearly lost it at that moment. What if someone had found out that Andrew and Andrea were his children and was now holding them for ransom? Many people knew that the Chesters were one of the wealthiest families in Montana. They were easy targets if anyone wanted to hatch a kidnapping plot. That's why all of them, including his sisters-in-law always had to be cautious and alert about their surroundings. Strangers who stepped on Moonbeam Ranch found themselves facing serious questions and sanctions. Harvey had gone a step further to ensure that all his family members were watched by guards whenever they were outside the compound.

His brothers' wives also had no idea that there were private detectives working on the ranch as cowhands. It was something all five of them had come up with just after their mother's death, when they realized how vulnerable they were. The work of the detectives was to make sure that nothing harmful befell anyone who lived or worked on the ranch. Any slight threat was dealt with seriously before it became a matter of concern. The men who drove the three family buggies had all served in the army and were well trained enough to guard the family members. Harvey took his position as head of the family very seriously and left nothing to chance!

Harvey blamed himself for whatever had happened to his children. His own foolishness had endangered his children. Had he gone for his family before this, his children would be safe now.

"We can't sit here talking and doing nothing. Let's begin the search before nightfall," Jesse said. "George, go and inform the sheriff while I go and get some of our cowboys to ride around. No one will rest until my niece and nephew are found."

∽

SALLY WAS weak from all the crying, and Harvey asked Lauren and Charlie to take care of her. But she too wanted to go out there and search for her children.

"Peace, be still," Charlie whispered. "The Lord is watching over your children, and they'll be safe, Sally. His promise in Psalm one hundred and twenty-one, verses seven and eight, is that He shall preserve us from all evil; He shall preserve our souls. The Lord shall preserve our going out and coming in from this time forth and forevermore. Andrew and Andrea are safe because the Lord is watching over them. Their lives are preserved."

Though Sally nodded at Charlie's gentle and comforting words, Sophie could see how distraught she was. She asked for some warm milk to be brought and when Sally wasn't looking, mixed some laudanum in it and gave her to drink. Sally fell asleep almost immediately, much to Harvey's and everyone else's relief. They were all concerned about the missing children but as their mother, Sally was the most affected. Her tears and pain were ripping at everyone's hearts, and they all needed to have clear heads to search for the twins. Emotions were high, and that wouldn't help the children. Everyone needed to calm down, and with Sally finally asleep, they could think rationally.

Harvey carried her to his room and Sophie followed. He laid her gently on the bed and covered her with a thick quilt, then stood beside the bed looking down at her.

"You really love her," Sophie observed, and Harvey nodded.

"I've been a fool and I blame myself for what has happened."

"How?"

"Had I brought my wife and children back home long ago, they wouldn't have been vulnerable. What if someone is holding my children captive and wants ransom. Well, ransom isn't the problem because I'm ready to do whatever it takes to have my children back."

"Harvey," Sophie placed a light hand on his arm. "The Lord is in control of this situation. We must believe that, or we'll lose our minds. We're people who believe in the power of prayer, and that's what we should do. We should pray and hold onto God's promises. The Lord will bring the children back home safely."

Harvey blinked and nodded, gently tapping Sophie's hand. "Thank you," his voice cracked. "I needed to hear those comforting words. Shall we join the rest in the living room?"

Harvey was feeling drained and was glad when his brother Jesse quickly organized a large search party of their workers. Jesse barked out instructions, and men rode in all directions in search of the twins. One cowboy came up with the idea of using a couple or so of the sheepdogs in the search. It wasn't unusual for them to use the dogs to search for missing animals or even children sometimes. Whenever floods or other disasters occurred and there was danger to mankind and beasts, after the Indian trackers, sheepdogs were the best searchers and had saved many lives in the past.

Giles Howard took the hound assigned to him and rode all the way toward Ennis, something making him take an unusual path. This particular path wandered from the main road toward the river and was sometimes used when one needed to water their horse along the journey to and from Ennis. Sometimes people used the bridge to cross over to the other side of town when they needed a shortcut and didn't want to have to use the long, well-paved road.

He was riding while the dog ran excitedly ahead of him, and the happy barking at the mouth of an open cave close to the river made him stop. He peered inside, and there he found two children fast asleep. From the description Harvey had given them of the twins, Giles was sure that these were the missing children. The little boy, Andrew had his arm around his sister as if to keep her safe.

Giles didn't want to frighten the children, but they looked cold, so he took his thick woolen blanket and covered them. Then he whispered a command for his dog to stay to watch over the children while he rode fast and hard to find Harvey or any of his brothers.

Harvey rode like the wind as soon as Giles told him about finding the children in the cave. He soon got to the cave and felt weakness overcome him. The children were awake and playing with Giles's dog. He was surprised to see a blanket neatly folded and placed beside the children. Giles quickly explained that it was his and he'd used it to cover the children when he'd found them sleeping.

It was Andrea who spotted Harvey first and gave him a smile that nearly brought him to his knees.

"Andrew, see, it's Papa," she said happily. "He came just like you said he would."

"Papa?" Andrew's eyes widened. "Where have you been? Mama used to have a big picture of you in our room, but she hid it from us. She's been very sad all these years. We came to find you, but Andrea got thirsty, so we came to find the river because we wanted to drink some water. Then we felt very tired and slept. When we woke up, we found this dog. God covered us with a blanket," he said, and the two adults chuckled.

"Well, you could say that Uncle Giles here was sent by God to cover you with his blanket."

"Thank you, Uncle Giles," Andrea petted the dog, which was like a kitten in the hands of the twins. Harvey knew that this particular hound was very fierce and one of their best sheep dogs. Yet here it was, playing with the children as if it were a house pet. "Papa, we woke up and found this dog watching over us. Papa, can we keep him please?"

Harvey threw his head back and laughed, going down on his haunches and holding out his arms for his children. They both walked into them without any hesitation at all, and the moment he held their warm little bodies, Harvey felt the tears filling his eyes, and he allowed them to fall unashamedly. Giles picked up his blanket and nodded at Harvey, then left. Now that the children were safely with their father, his work here was done. The dog would easily find its way back home, and in any case, Harvey would make sure it returned safely to the ranch. With a quick wave he was gone.

"Papa, are you crying? Are you hurt?" Andrea pulled back and looked into her father's face. She went so far as to wipe his face. "Papa, please don't cry. Let's go and find Mama so she can make you feel better."

"Yes, Papa," Mama always makes us feel better when we're sad. We want to go home to Mama."

"I'll take you home to see Mama," Harvey rose to his feet again. "Come, let's go home and see your Mama."

"Papa, can we please keep this dog? I like him very much," Andrew insisted.

"I like this dog, too, Papa. Let us keep him," Andrea piped in.

Harvey couldn't get enough of his children, and he held onto their hands. "This dog belongs to Uncle Giles, but I promise you that you'll each get a puppy of your own."

The happy screams nearly deafened his ears, but he didn't care. The twins could shout as loud as they wanted, for they were with their father now! Harvey had feared that his children might be afraid of him or reject him because he was a stranger to them. After Giles had told him that the twins had been found, he'd prayed so hard that they wouldn't refuse to come with him. Children he'd seen only from a distance and who didn't know him might be scared when they first met him, he'd thought.

Yet here they were, and they'd accepted him as if they'd always been with him, and he knew that it was because of Sally. He owed his wife so much and purposed then and there that he would do everything he could to restore his family. He owed a huge debt of gratitude to Sally, and God helping him, he would do all he could to repay it.

"Dear Lord, please help me and have mercy on us. Please soften Sally's heart so she'll agree to return as my wife. I don't deserve anything, and all I ask for is your mercy."

Harvey refused to let go of his children's hands, and they skipped at his side as he led them to where he'd tethered his horse. The dog ran behind them and waited patiently beside Harvey's horse as he placed the children on it. Then Harvey got on, and he was careful not to ride too fast even though he wanted to get home as fast as he could. He knew that Sally would be out of her mind if she woke up and her children hadn't been found yet. It was late in the afternoon and darkness would soon descend on the land. He wanted the twins back home where it was warm and safe.

"This is not the way to our home," Andrew said, looking around him in wonder as they rode through the large ranch gates and down the beautifully cobbled driveway. "Papa, where is this place?"

"This, my son, is your real home where you and your Mama will live with me forever."

HIS MISSING FAMILY

Harvey was holding the hands of his children when Sally entered the living room. She gasped and nearly collapsed in relief. Her children were safe, and they were standing on either side of their father, holding his hands. They looked so contented in Harvey's presence that she felt a pang of guilt for having kept them apart for this long.

As soon as the twins spied their mother they broke away from their father and rushed toward her.

Sally knelt down and held both arms wide open.

"Mama," Andrew got to her first, and his sister joined them.

"My darling babies," Sally held her children close.

Harvey stood there looking at his wife and children, and a lump formed in his throat. He'd lost seven years of his wife and children's lives and didn't know if Sally would ever forgive him. He'd let her down and not protected them, leaving them vulnerable to any and all dangers. It was just by the mercies of God that his family had remained safe all this while. Now he would always be there for his family.

"Mama, see our Papa. He's just like your picture. He came to find us," Andrew reported to his mother. "He was crying, and we told him that you would make him feel better."

"Is that right now?" Sally raised her eyes up to Harvey, laughter dancing in her eyes. She could now afford to smile and be happy because her children had been found. "Why was Papa crying?"

Andrea shrugged as if she didn't care because all she felt now was happiness at seeing her Mama once again.

"You little rascals really had me worried," Sally held her children close until they squealed in protest.

"Mama, you're holding me too tight," Andrew wriggled.

"Let go, Mama," Andrea added her voice.

Sally reluctantly let go of the twins and they helped her to her feet. Then they squeezed themselves against her, and Sally realized that they were feeling shy because of the number of people around them. Harvey's brothers and their wives were all standing around the living room staring at the twins in wonderment, and Sally smiled because she knew her children were overwhelmed.

"As I live and breathe," Walter finally spoke up, and his voice was full of awe. "Harvey, how is it that we've never met our nephew and niece before now? I remember Sally, but this is all so amazing, that you're married and have children together."

Harvey smiled at his brother. "Walter, it's a long story and one I'll tell you at some point. For now, I want to get my children and wife settled in. They need to freshen up and have something to eat, then rest. They've all had a long day indeed."

∼

Sally was surprised when Harvey led her back to his bedroom and not one of the guestrooms. She'd woken up in this room moments ago before she knew that the children had been found. It even surprised her that she'd fallen asleep amid all the turmoil that was going on around them.

"What am I doing here? I should be with my children."

"My love, Andrea and Andrew are in good hands with Glenda. Her twin sisters will keep our children busy and happy. After you've rested, you'll go and see them in the nursery."

"Who's Glenda?"

"You already saw her in the living room, but the excitement of finding the twins was too much, and I'm sorry I didn't introduce you to the rest of the family. Glenda is Joe's wife. Then Walter has Lauren, George has Sophie and Jesse is married to Charlie."

"Yes, Jess already introduced me to Charlie, and I met Lauren and Sophie too." She smiled. "Seems like this was the year of marriages for the Chester brothers," Sally said without malice. "I'm very happy for your brothers because they've found love with very wonderful women. I spent some time with Lauren, Charlie, and Sophie and found them to be really kind and understanding. They're a blessing to be with."

"We've been blessed," Harvey said. "Even I who was separated from my wife for seven years have seen the goodness of the Lord."

"And whose fault was it that you were estranged from your own wife and children?" Sally turned and looked at him. "When your mother threatened me…"

"Wait, what did you say? My mother threatened you?" Harvey was shocked to hear that. But then he told himself that he shouldn't be surprised at his mother's actions at all. Many years ago, just after their father's death, his mother had gotten involved with Mr. Russell, who turned out to be Glenda's father.

Not only had Owen Russell been younger than their mother but he'd been married at the time, and his wife was expecting their first child. It was just recently that they'd found all this out, when Joe was searching for some old ranch journals and came across some love letters. These had been written to their mother by Mr. Russell. Because of his mother, Mr. Russell had sent his wife and unborn child away.

So, nothing about his mother's doings surprised him anymore. He'd always seen her as a very pious and straightforward woman, but he was finding out that she was different from the person he'd always thought she was. She'd fallen off the pedestal he and his brothers had long placed her on!

Sally was surprised when her husband fell silent and even failed to defend his mother like he'd always done in the past. He seemed to be lost in thought, so she sat on the large chair in his room and leaned back, observing his every move.

"Is anything the matter?" She finally asked when the silence became too lengthy.

Harvey sighed, "I should have known that Mama was behind your leaving. At the time, she mentioned that you'd just run away, and I didn't once question her." He walked to her and crouched beside the chair. "Sally, losing you was the worst time of my life. I never thought I could go on. I never knew that Mama threatened you in any way."

"She said if I didn't leave Moonbeam Ranch—in fact, she wanted me gone from Beaverhead completely—that she would make sure she got rid of me and my baby."

"What?" Harvey had to sit down because his knees suddenly felt weak.

"Yes. I was scared for my life and had to run as fast as I could to escape her wrath. Only I expected that you would come looking for me."

"I wanted to but got caught up in so many things, especially after Mama died."

"But you had the chance to find us after your mother passed away. You knew that the only place I would seek refuge was at the church. It was Jesse who found me walking on the road after your mother sent me away and took me to the church. The reverend found me the teaching position in Butte and just recently recommended me for the new posting in Ennis. Had you wanted to, you'd have so easily found us."

"You're right, and I feel deeply ashamed of myself, Sally. But I was afraid."

"What could you have been afraid of?"

"That you wouldn't want to see me or have anything to do with me after I'd let you down. I knew I'd disappointed and failed you, so I was ashamed to face you. I couldn't take the thought of you rejecting me, Sally; it would have finished me. It was easier for me to keep hoping that one day I'd wake up and you'd be back here with our children."

Sally couldn't believe that this big, strong man was afraid of anything. Yet when she looked into his eyes, she saw vulnerability there. His eyes showed that he'd suffered as much, if not more than she had at their separation. At least she'd had their children, but Harvey had had no one save for his brothers, and that was different.

"Sally, for the sake of our children, please forgive me and my mother for whatever we did to you. Please show us your mercy."

FAMILY IS EVERYTHING

The atmosphere in the house was lively as the twins were passed around the living room. They were well rested, and it was the second day since their arrival on Moonbeam Ranch. Their uncles were so happy as were their new aunts, and the twins were in their element.

Sally allowed the tears to fall as she watched her children being received into their father's family. She'd stayed away too long! Her anger and selfishness had denied her children the chance to know their family before this, and she felt deeply ashamed of herself. Hadn't the pastor once preached about never allowing the root of bitterness to grow deep in one's heart because it caused nothing but pain and regrets? Yet she'd allowed herself to harbor unforgiveness in her heart for so many years. She just prayed that her children would never hold this against her when they came of age and understood that for the first six years of their lives, they'd lived without their father.

Harvey had arranged for this special luncheon when everyone was rested after the ordeal of the previous day and the whole family could be together.

Andrea and Andrew moved around the room with Alicia and Alison. The two sets of twins had bonded so well and were now fast friends. Sally saw the deep love that the five brothers shared, and which had now been extended to their wives. This was one big, happy family and she almost felt like an intruder.

"My love, why do you have tears in your eyes? Our children are so happy, and see the happiness on my brothers' faces. They all worried about me after they got married, and seeing you and the twins has calmed their hearts. This was long overdue and I'm sorry that I didn't act sooner."

Sally was done blaming her husband because he, too, had been under his mother's control and manipulation. While she was still hurt that he'd never come to look for them, she acknowledged that for the sake of her children, she needed to forgive their father. Forgiving Mrs. Chester was another issue altogether, and she'd have to pray for special grace for that. But it wasn't something she wanted to deal with right now.

"You're not saying anything," Harvey was worried because he had no idea what his wife was thinking right now. What if she decided to leave now that the children had been found? He couldn't imagine spending another single day away from his lovely wife and children.

As he watched them being fussed over by his brothers and their wives, Harvey realized that his children fit right in.

"I'm just watching Andrea and Andrew," Sally said with a soft sigh. "If anyone was to walk into this house, even a total stranger to the family, they would believe it if they were told that the twins have always lived here among their family. They're so much at home that it even looks as if they were born here."

Harvey's lips tightened, "They should have been born here in their home; and you're right, they belong here. Had I been a better husband to you and paid more attention to whatever was happening at home, things wouldn't have become so bad that you had to leave home because of fear. I would not have missed out on the first six years of my children's lives. I'd have been there with you through the months you were carrying them. I'd have been there when they were born and cut their first teeth. I missed their first steps and hearing them speak their first words."

Harvey looked so sad that Sally was moved. "Andrea's first word was '*da, da*' and Andrew said '*ma, ma*' first." She smiled in fond remembrance. "It was Andrew who crawled first, but Andrea overtook him and walked before him. They were good babies and gave me no trouble at all. Some women from the church in Butte surrounded me with so much love and acceptance that I forgot all my pain and sorrow for a time." She looked at him. "We were never alone, Harvey."

"Thank you so much for trying to make me feel better. I understand if you're angry with me but thank you for staying calm under the circumstances. If I could turn back the hands of time, I would do so and make so many changes to the decisions that I made then."

Sally shrugged, "What's been done is past and there's no point crying over spilt milk. I have to find a way to get over all the anger that is within me for the sake of our children," she shook her head. "I can't believe that these two rascals decided to leave home and find their way to Beaverhead."

"Did you find out how they knew which road to follow or where to go?" Harvey asked. He still got the shivers when he thought about the danger his children had been in. "The Lord really protected our children for us. It's going to be a while before I stop shaking whenever I think about them walking all alone on that road. Hardly anyone uses it anymore, which is both a

good and bad thing. Good in the sense that they didn't attract anyone's attention and bad because had they gotten into trouble there would have been no one to help them."

"I asked them how they thought of coming to Beaverhead," Sally laughed. "Those children of yours are just something else."

"What did they say?" Harvey was interested in what his wife had to tell him.

"They were searching for something in one of my drawers after we moved and happened to find my newest journal. And they took it upon themselves to read it."

"What?"

Sally nodded. "From the day I left Moonbeam Ranch, I started keeping a journal of my life so that one day I would share it with my children. I told myself that one day they would ask about their father and how they were born, where they were born, who their larger family is, and all that. So, I made sure that every day I made an entry in the journal, and over the years, I've collected a number of those."

Harvey chuckled softly, "Don't tell me they read through seven years of your journals."

"No, they only found the most recent one. When we moved from Butte, I boxed all the old stuff so only my latest journal was available. That's the one they read and got on the road to Beaverhead," she looked at Harvey. "I made the mistake of showing them the road leading to Beaverhead from Ennis, and they remembered. You gave me such intelligent children that I'm almost afraid of who they'll become when they grow up. I'm afraid of what they'll do then. They're only six and yet think like adults. If those two ever get onto a train engine, you can be sure that they'll do all they can to convince the engineer to let them drive it."

Harvey was laughing, and Sally's breath caught in her throat. He was so handsome and looked much younger. He lapped up all the stories she told him about their children and the milestones they'd achieved so far. Harvey knew that for as long as he lived, he'd never tire of hearing about his children's escapades and adventures.

"Just last summer the twins decided that they would paint our house in Butte."

"Really?"

Sally nodded, grinning at her husband. She'd yearned for moments like this when she would share stories about their children with him. In the past they hadn't shared such closeness because his mother had done all she could to keep them apart. "Yes Harvey, your children saw whitewash in a barrel in the shed at the back of the house and decided that they could do a better job than the painter. Mr. Foster, the painter, said they did a good job at least as far as they could reach. And I agreed with him. One thing about the twins is that they're fast learners and when they set their minds to do something, they perfect it. I decided that they were ready to learn how to ride and was going to find them a place on one of the small farms in Ennis. That's another reason I moved there when the chance arose." She looked intensely at Harvey. "I knew that one day they would come back home to Moonbeam, so I needed them to be well prepared."

"Thank you," Harvey whispered, feeling overwhelmed by Sally's words. She was a good mother, and it gladdened his heart to know that she'd anticipated that one day her children would return to Moonbeam where they belonged.

"Why are you thanking me?"

"For being a wonderful mother to our children," he took a shaky breath. "For telling them about me even when I wasn't there. Andrew, or was it Andrea, told me that you had a big picture of me but now hid it from them."

Sally covered her face in embarrassment. "It was the only thing of yours that I decided to take with me when I left. I told myself that one day your children would want to know who their father was and what he looked like. When they were younger, I had it pinned on the wall between their beds, so yours was the first face they saw when they woke up and the last one before they fell asleep. But as they grew older and started asking too many questions about you, I decided to take it down and hide it."

"Why weren't they in school yesterday? I believe school term is in session right now."

"Yes, it is, but with the approaching winter, the pastor decided to carry out renovations on the two schoolrooms. So, he gave us all a two-week holiday, which started the day before yesterday."

~

WHEREAS SALLY HAD INITIALLY BEEN ANNOYED at the interruption in the school semester, she was now glad that she didn't have to run all over the place seeking permission to be away from the classroom and her students. The two-week hiatus forced on them by the pastor was proving to be a blessing in disguise. But it would end, and she'd have to return to Ennis. What would happen then, she wondered.

Now that the twins had tasted the goodness of being around their father and his family, she knew it wouldn't be easy to take them away. And she found that she didn't want to. Her children belonged here, and she wanted the best for them. Yet she had an obligation to continue serving as a teacher because she'd made that commitment to the school where she taught.

"Oh Lord," she prayed. "Please show me what to do."

NEW SISTERS

"It was his mother who sent you away?" Lauren stared at Sally in astonishment. "I can't believe that our mother-in-law would do such a terrible thing to her own son's wife."

Sally nodded as she sat in a chair and leaned onto the kitchen table.

"Mrs. Chester never wanted me to be her son's wife, and we got married against her wishes. I was so young and scared and with no one to guide me," Sally said. "The aunt who would have helped me at the time had passed away, and I was left all alone with only Harvey and his mother. His brothers were too young to know whatever was going on and had been told that I was just a servant. We hid our marriage from them, and only Jesse suspected that there was more to our relationship than what he'd been told. When Mrs. Chester told me that she would kill me and my unborn child, well children, I believed her and ran for my life."

"I do believe that our mother-in-law would do such a thing," Glenda said. "She was the cause of my parents' broken marriage and why I never knew who my father was. I came to know of my father after my mother's death when she asked me to come and find him. She thought he was still alive. Mr. Owen Russell died just before our mother-in-law did."

"Yes," Sophie nodded. "George told me something of the sort. It was Joe who found out about the illicit relationship when he got some of the love letters in our mother-in-law's trunks. Apparently, Mrs. Chester had a long-term relationship with Mr. Russell, who was Glenda's father."

Lauren looked at Sophie in shock. "Walter also mentioned something about his mother and some scandal, but I never paid any attention to whatever he was saying."

"How did you cope with two children all on your own?" Charlie asked. "It must have been very hard."

Sally nodded, "When I left this ranch, my heart was so bitter toward my husband and his mother. But as soon as the twins came, I began to feel pity for them. Harvey and his mother may have been wealthy in material things but not in what really mattered. I had the twins and their love. Harvey and his mother were missing out on spending time with these special children. When I heard that my mother-in-law had passed away, I expected that Harvey would come to find us, but he never did. So, I stopped thinking about our marriage, or I told myself so. Mrs. Chester wanted him to marry a woman of their social standing and not a nonentity like me, so I told myself that it didn't matter at all. But my heart broke each time I thought about Harvey finding someone else and moving on with his life while forgetting about me and our children."

"Do you think Mama Chester would have accepted any one of us as her daughter-in-law?" Lauren's gaze went around the kitchen. "She's beginning to sound like she was a very difficult person to please. Would any of us have attained to the standards she'd set for her sons' wives?"

"None of us, well apart from Sally, ever got to know her," Sophie said. "It's sad that she missed out on her firstborn grandchildren. She'll never get to see any of the generations after her own children."

"From what I gather, probably only Sophie might have been accepted by Mrs. Chester," Charlie said. "The rest of us would have been treated as badly as Sally was."

"We don't know that." Lauren was willing to give their mother-in-law the benefit of the doubt. "Maybe if she'd lived, she would have changed and accepted that love doesn't choose where to grow."

There were murmurs around the table, but the other four women had their doubts about Mrs. Chester mellowing enough to allow her sons to make their own choices of brides.

"This may sound a little harsh, but I believe that God works all things together for the good of those who love Him," Glenda said. "Our husbands are good men, and it would have been terrible for them if they'd been forced to marry the women chosen for them, instead of the ones they loved. Now I finally understand why Harvey always looked lost and sad. He would be smiling, yes, but his eyes always showed sadness and pain. None of us could have guessed that he had a family out there."

The five women sat in silence as they watched over the four children and four puppies frolicking on the kitchen floor.

"Let's not be gloomy," Sophie said, and Sally turned to look at her. "I'm saying this not to hurt anyone but so we can think deeply about it."

The other four looked at her expectantly.

"Mrs. Chester was who she was, and in her lifetime she made many mistakes. But let's also remember that she gave us five fine men who are now our husbands. I'm thinking that for their sakes and for our children not yet born and yet to be brought into this world, let's forgive her."

"She isn't here to hear what we have to say even when we're forgiving her," Lauren said.

Sophie nodded, "I know that our mother-in-law isn't here but we can still forgive and release her from our hearts. I know that there are many things she did that may have affected our husbands both in good and bad ways. Let's ask for forgiveness for their sake and show mercy to her. That's the only way we'll be able to move past all this."

Sally looked down and thought about what Sophie had said. She realized that she wanted to continue holding onto her anger toward Mrs. Chester. Her mother-in-law had caused her to lose seven years of her marriage. She'd caused her children to miss out on seven years of their father's love and attention.

But Sophie was right; she needed to forgive and let go. For the sake of her children and the man she was still in love with, her heart needed to be empty of bitterness and anger. Holding grudges only made life worse and not better for anyone. The only question is whether they were both ready to start all over again. It all depended on Harvey.

"Sally, you're not saying anything," Lauren said.

"Perhaps this might help," Glenda spoke up and all eyes turned to her. "When Joe and I got married, I wanted to put my pain away and be happy. I realized that unless I forgave my father and Mrs. Chester for the role they had played in breaking up my Mama's happiness and marriage, I would never move on. Being angry meant that I would end up carrying pain and bringing it into my marriage, and thus cause my innocent husband to suffer. So, I asked my husband on our wedding day itself to take me to visit the public cemetery. That's where my father is buried, and thereafter to the family graveyard up the hill. I knew that Mrs. Chester and my father were both dead, but standing by their graves and forgiving them brought me much inner peace. I was able to forgive the two people who'd wronged me so badly and caused me to never know my father." Glenda smiled at Sally especially. "It might help for you to visit Mrs. Chester's grave and have a lengthy talk as if you were face to face with her. Pour your heart out even if she's not there to hear you. The Lord will listen, and He'll provide the balm you need for your soul and wounded heart."

Sally thought about it, and what Glenda said made a lot of sense. She was tired of being in pain and carrying bitterness within her heart. She could never move forward unless she went back to the past and released her heart.

Harvey approached the women from one side of the portico, and after greeting them all he turned to his wife.

"Love, may I have a word with you?"

Sally nodded and rose to her feet. She took the hand he held out to her and ignored the knowing looks from her sisters-by-marriage. In them she'd found soulmates and sisters, something she'd never had before. This was her family, and for the first time, she felt the joy of belonging to others fill her heart.

"There's something I want to show you," Harvey said when they were away from the others. He took her to the corral where there were two beautiful white ponies.

"I got them for Andrea and Andrew," he announced, moving closer to the two animals, which stood close together as if they were afraid. Harvey gently stroked their backs. "They're very docile and the best kind for children to learn how to ride on. What do you think?"

"They're beautiful and so white," Sally blinked rapidly to dispel her tears. "The twins will be so happy."

"They won't always be white," Harvey told her. "When they grow up, their coats will change. There's also a nice mare you can ride. You used to be a good rider, and I hope you still remember how to get onto a horse."

"But what happens when we return to Ennis? I have an obligation to my students, and my house doesn't have a stable close by where the horses can stay. Also, once school is in session, I always get too busy, and then who'll look after the ponies?"

Harvey shook his head, "Sally, I'm never letting you go again. I lost too much in the past and I'm not prepared for a life of loneliness and pain again."

"But..."

"You and my children belong right here with me. You also need to realize that your safety is paramount, so I'll escort you to Ennis so you can pack up and move to Moonbeam Ranch. We'll speak to the pastor who is patron of the school, and I'm sure he'll understand that a wife needs to be with her husband, and children with their father. Also, if you must continue teaching at the school, I'll provide you with a buggy to take you to and from the place. But my children will remain here, and you'll go to school from this ranch."

"Harvey, you're being too rigid. I know that Ennis is only about four or five miles from this place but travelling to and from each morning and evening will take its toll on the horse and buggy driver."

Harvey gave her a tight smile, "There's a reason we pay wages to people, and that's for them to work. Most of the time the buggies stay idle as do some of the stable boys. It will be good for them to move around a little and not get lazy. Besides, it will only be for a short time as you give the school notice so they can find a replacement for you. After that I'm sure you'll be able to find a position in one of the schools here in Beaverhead."

Sally nodded and sighed. She sensed that if it was up to him, Harvey would never let her or the children out of his sight again.

IN HIS ARMS

***A** Few Days Later*

"Sally, you've done an amazing job with our children," Harvey told her as they sat together in the parlor. The twins were somewhere around the ranch with one of his brothers. "They're not only adorable, but Andrew and Andrea are confident and intelligent. Most of all, they're happy, secure children, brought up by a strong mother." He shook his head. "How will I ever make up for all the time I lost?"

Sally gave him a small tight smile. "You're here now, and the twins loved you before they ever met you. Please just be the father they need, and don't let them down again."

Harvey knelt in front of Sally and took both her hands in his. "Sally, I promise that God helping me, I'll never let the three of you leave me again."

Their gazes locked and held, and Sally felt like crying. This is what she'd prayed and cried for, and now that it was happening, she felt as if it was all a dream.

"Am I dreaming?" She whispered to herself, but Harvey heard her.

"No, my love, this is no dream. Now we need to travel to Ennis so we can gather all your belongings and bring them here."

"But what about my work as a teacher? Harvey, I love what I do, and sharing my knowledge with children is something I believe I was born to do. This is my purpose in life, and I don't want to stop teaching the little ones."

"And you won't," Harvey reassured her. "Our church has started a mission school and teachers are needed. There are other schools in this town as well. You could always get a teaching position in one of the schools, because I also intend for us to enroll the twins right here in Beaverhead. Like I said, for the moment you can carry on teaching in Ennis while they look for your replacement. We will speak to the schools in Beaverhead to see if they'll offer you a position. My inclination is toward our mission school, but whatever comes up will be all right with me."

Sally felt relieved that her husband had no intention of stopping her from teaching. She wasn't doing it for the money but because it was her greatest desire to provide knowledge to young minds. She wasn't the kind of person who would be contented with just sitting at home taking care of a husband and children. She needed to use her brain to do more.

"Once you've settled down, we'll go to the Reverend and make your application. Good thing is that you have vast experience, so you stand a very good chance of obtaining a position for yourself."

"Thank you."

"Don't thank me just yet. At least wait until everything is in place first."

"I'm hopeful."

∼

Since it wasn't long that Sally had moved from Butte to Ennis, most of their things were still packed up. It was easy to transport everything, and soon Sally was settled in her new home. And just as Harvey had predicted, the pastor was only too happy to hear that Sally was reconciling with her husband, and he gave them his blessings. He also expressed gratitude that she would be willing to carry on teaching at the school until a replacement was found.

"It's good to have you here," Harvey told her. "I really want you to be my wife again, Sally."

"Why? Because of the twins?"

"No, because I love you, Sally. Even without the twins, my love would still be deep and strong for you. I never stopped loving you and seeing you again has made me realize that I was only half alive without you."

"Harvey, we've been apart for seven years, and I need to be sure that our marriage will work before I make a commitment again. I'm here because it's important for our children to grow up around their father and in their home. This is where they belong, and I'll be here to see them grow." Sally sighed. "For now, let's just leave things as they are."

There was finality in her voice and Harvey was surprised at this new woman before him. In the past she'd have accepted everything he asked of her, sometimes even falling all over herself to do his bidding.

"That said," Sally continued, "You need to find me another room to use."

"But why? What's wrong with this one?"

"This is your bedroom, and I don't want to sleep in here with you."

"Sally, we're married," Harvey cried out in dismay. "Husbands and wives always share a room."

Sally gave him a thoughtful look, "We haven't lived together as a married couple for seven years. And besides, apart from the children we have, who knows that we actually got married legally? We had a very private and secret wedding, and I'm sure your brothers have a lot of questions about us," she moved to the other side of the room. "People will look at us as if we're living in sin. Do we even have any proof of our wedding? I remember that your mother tore up our marriage license. She said our marriage was null and void and meant nothing at all and that piece of paper was as cheap as trash."

Harvey looked down. Sally was right. His mother had ripped their marriage license to shreds in his presence, and as if that wasn't enough, she'd tossed the pieces into the fireplace.

"We could always get another license to replace the one Mama tore up. What?" He asked when Sally shook her head.

"You just don't get it, do you?" She said and walked out of the bedroom, leaving Harvey staring after her in shock.

∼

"Harvey, you look down in the dumps," Jesse walked into the study where Harvey was seated behind the large desk feeling very miserable. "What happened?" He took the chair on the other side of the desk.

"Jesse, I'm in pain," Harvey told his brother. "My heart is bleeding and I feel like it's been shredded to pieces."

"What happened, Harvey?"

"It's my wife. Sally has refused for us to live together as a married couple again. She says she's only here because of the twins."

"Why would she say that? It's obvious that she's still very much in love with you. I've seen how she looks at you. Why then would she refuse you?"

Harvey sighed, "Sally says that no one recognizes that we're married because we had a secret wedding, and Mama tore up our marriage license. She insists that no one will believe that we got married legally."

"Mama tore up your license?"

"Yes. She said that she didn't recognize our marriage and it was null and void. Sally says no one will believe we got married in the right way. I suggested that we get another license to replace that one and she got angry."

"And with good reason too, Harvey."

"Did I say something wrong?"

"Yes. Replacing that license means the wedding and marriage remain as a secret and that's not what Sally wants."

"What then should I do?" Harvey asked, quite perplexed.

"Very easy, my big Brother, there's something you can do to reassure your wife of your good intentions."

"Jesse, you're speaking in parables."

"Brother, just arrange to have another wedding—a proper one this time. Have a real wedding this time. Let Sally know that she means the world to you and you're not ashamed of her. She probably feels that you don't value her enough to let the whole world know that she's your wife."

And it was like his understanding was suddenly opened up, and Harvey smiled broadly. He slapped his hand hard on the desk, and Jesse winced. "My dear brother, you've just made my day a very happy one. Quick, what do we need to do to make this wedding happen and in the shortest and fastest time possible?"

Jesse chuckled, "Slow down, Cowboy! You have four brothers and four sisters who have all had weddings in the past eight months or so. We're well able to make these arrangements so that Sally gets the wedding she missed out on, and to bring the two of you together. Just say the word and all shall be done."

"I've just said it, Jesse. Go ahead and do whatever needs to be done." Jesse rose to his feet. "And Jesse?"

"Yes, Harvey?"

"No expense should be spared. Go all out and give my beautiful wife a wedding befitting the queen that she is."

"Remember that Christmas Day is approaching."

"What better time than this season of good will and glad tidings to complete the family?"

A CHRISTMAS DELIGHT

"Here you go," Harvey handed pieces of colored ribbon to the twins. "Let's go ahead and decorate our Christmas tree."

"Papa," Andrea gazed adoringly at her father. "This tree is bigger than the one we had last year."

"Yes, Papa," Andrew joined in, but his eyes were on his mother. "Mama said one day you'll come back and bring us a big tree."

"This is a big tree," Glenda walked into the living room with Alicia and Alison. The moment they caught sight of the tree, they forgot all about her and ran to where Andrea and Andrew were. In a short moment the living room was filled with happy shrieks as the four children ran around adding ribbons to the tree. The puppies also yapped happily and were careful not to get in the way of the humans in the living room.

Soon the tree looked very colorful, and the children clapped in delight.

Harvey's eyes moved to where Sally was. She had a lost look in her eyes and was staring at Glenda and Joe. When Walter and Lauren walked in holding hands, Harvey thought he saw the shimmer of tears in Sally's eyes.

Jesse's words returned to his mind. *"Have a real wedding this time. Let Sally know that she means the world to you and you're not ashamed of her. She probably feels that you don't value her enough to let the whole world know that she's your wife."*

A thought came to his mind, and it was as if there was a sudden burst of sunshine. He knew just what he was going to do.

∼

Christmas Day

"This is the right time to bring this up, when the whole family is gathered here together," Harvey stood at the head place of the dining table. "As the head of the family, I want to give thanks to the Lord our God for bringing us thus far." He looked around and smiled at everyone who was seated around the table. His brothers and their wives as well as the two sets of twins and Sally were present, as was Glenda's grandaunt.

"Last Christmas it was just the five of us, and we didn't imagine that a year later our lives would have changed so much." He smiled at his sisters-in-law. Then his gaze settled on Sally who was seated at his immediate right hand. "Then our Lord in His mercy brought these five beautiful and wonderful women into our lives. In the short span of just months, my brothers all found the women they loved and now our number is set to increase. Lauren and Walter are expecting, as are Joe and Glenda." His eyes settled on Alicia and Alison. "Glenda brought us much happiness when she her sisters and Aunt Zippy joined us to make this family grow. Then Sally, the love of my life, added to that happiness by bringing Andrea and Andrew to us."

"You said it, Brother," Joe clapped his hands.

"Lauren, Sophie, Charlie, and Glenda, you've all given my brothers so much peace and happiness, and I'm so happy that you're all a part of this family." Harvey rang the small bell, and their new housekeeper walked in carrying a tray on which were five dark blue velvet boxes. She handed them over to Harvey. He placed them side by side on the table in front of him.

"Before Mama died, she handed over all her jewelry worth thousands of dollars to the five of us. She made us promise that when we got married, we'd share the jewelry equally among our five brides." His brothers nodded. "A few days ago, when Sally and my children joined the family, my brothers and I sat down and realized that it was time for all our brides to receive the gifts Mama left for them, and what better time than now to give them to our brides. Christmas Day is the time to give gifts."

Harvey handed out the boxes to the five women. Sally received hers with much trepidation. She couldn't believe she was receiving something that once belonged to the woman who'd detested her so much. She nearly laughed out loud at the irony of it all. Mrs. Chester would never have given her a single piece of jewelry, not in a hundred years. Yet here she was now in possession of the woman's own priceless jewelry.

"And one more thing," Harvey moved closer to Sally then knelt before her. Every eye was on the two of them.

"This ring was given to me by our grandmother. As a matter of fact, she gave rings to all five of us," he looked around and his brothers nodded. "Mama was present when our grandmother handed over the rings to us, and she took them and kept them for us. I asked Mama for mine when I wanted to make you my wife," he twisted his lips and shook her head. "Mama refused to get the ring from the safety deposit box because she didn't want me to give it to you, my only bride for as long as I live. I only got it after Mama had passed away, but by then you'd already gone from my life. Still, I held onto it because I knew that one day, you would return to me and wear it forever for me." He held the ring up to the light and it glowed like a star.

"Salome Angela Chester, would you be my bride again? Would you be the woman of my heart for the rest of my life? Will you be my companion to laugh and cry with, to share the good and the bad things that life will bring us? Will you walk this journey called life with me?"

Sally was shedding tears, and she thought her heart would burst open because it was overflowing with so much love and happiness. This is what she'd prayed for. Harvey was acknowledging her openly before his family and expressing his love for her. This was an answer to her prayers.

"My Love," Harvey reached forward and used his thumb to wipe her tears. "I love you so much and want the whole world to know it. My darling, I'm going to wed you again in the biggest ceremony Beaverhead has ever seen. By the grace of God, our wedding will be spoken of for many years to come. Every eye will see me marrying you properly, and every ear present will hear how much I love you, Sally. You're my love, my treasure, my world, and I'm so deeply in love with you."

Sally found herself on her knees and in her husband's arms.

"I love you so much Harvey, and yes, I'll be your bride and love you for the rest of my life."

"Welcome home, my love."

GRAND FINALE

A soft, warm breeze fluttered Sally's veil, which Sophie had just placed on her head.

"Oh my," Lauren who'd just walked in whispered. "I've never seen such a beautiful and glowing bride in my life before."

"She truly looks adorable and amazing," Sophie agreed.

"And it's all thanks to you, my lovely sisters," Sally said with tears in her eyes. "I could not have asked for such loving and kind sisters. Thank you all so much for doing this for me."

"You'll walk into the new year with a whole new life before you," Glenda said.

"He makes all things beautiful in His time," Charlie whispered.

Sally agreed with Charlie. Just when she'd thought that nothing good could come her way, the Lord did it for her, and here she was, about to walk down the aisle and into the arms of the man she loved with her whole heart.

Someone knocked at the door, and before any of the women could say anything, it was pushed open, and Joe stuck his head into the room. "If we don't leave in the next one minute, Harvey will collapse into a pool of water. Jesse just returned from church, and the poor fellow is as nervous as the bride," he peered at Sally. "In fact, you are holding up better than my brother."

Sally smiled at him, "That's because my sisters have surrounded me with their love and prayers. But you're right, I know that Harvey is very nervous right now, and I believe I'm ready."

"Good girl," Joe applauded, and they left the house for the church soon after.

Harvey's chest tightened when he saw the twins, his own children, walking down the aisle toward him. Andrew was carrying a Bible, while Andrea had a small basket filled with petals. At Lauren's directive she was sprinkling a few petals on the floor.

These adorable children who'd won the hearts of everyone who saw them were his offspring. He felt proud and humbled at the same time.

"Thank You, Lord, for being so good and gracious to me," he whispered even as he looked toward the door and saw his bride standing there. Then his eyes met Jesse's, and they expressed his silent gratitude for advising him to do this.

Yes, every woman deserved a beautiful wedding, so her husband could show her off to the world. Every bride deserved to be publicly acknowledged by her groom so that people would respect her.

Sally felt like she was floating as she glided down the aisle toward the man who'd won her heart years ago.

It was one of the best weddings that Beaverhead had ever seen and would be talked of for years to come.

"My wife, at last," Harvey said when they were on their way back to the ranch for their reception. "I love you so much, Sally. This is what I should have done years ago if I hadn't been such a cowardly fellow. I missed you more than anything, my darling. Thank you for coming back into my life and enriching it."

"I missed you so much, too," Sally said. "It broke my heart to think that you were probably married to another."

"Never would I have married another woman, Sally. You're my world, and I kept my eyes on you all these years. Wherever you went, I was a step ahead of you, making the path clear and comfortable because if I couldn't have you with me, at least I could love you from afar."

"What?"

"Yes, my Love. Many times, I came close to revealing my presence to you and the twins, but guilt and fear kept me away. I always told myself that you were better off without me because I was a weak man."

"No, please don't say that," Sally leaned closer to her husband. Then something struck her. "Are you saying that you provided for us all that time?" The guilty and cheeky look that she'd seen on the faces of her children gave her the answer she sought, and she giggled. "No wonder the Pastor was always so eager and willing to provide for us. I always said that he was a thoughtful and selfless man who denied himself and looked after us. So, you were giving him money for us?"

Harvey nodded, "I wanted to make sure that my family was well provided for. And Pastor kept his word to never let you know that I was always there in the background watching over you and our children."

Sally was silent for a moment.

"Thank you," she said at last. "Harvey, you're a good man and I love you even more."

"My sunshine and rain of blessings," he whispered.

"There's something that I need to do," Sally told her husband.

"What's that?"

"It was actually Glenda's idea." She told him about Glenda's visit to the family graveyard to ask for forgiveness and to also release herself from the bitterness she'd carried toward his mother for all these years.

"We can go there right now," Harvey said, and they did so.

Sally spent nearly ten minutes at the graveside, and Harvey let her be.

She stood beside the grave and looked down at the grassy mound and sighed. "It's very strange that we all live our lives hating people, being prejudiced, and looking down on each other. Life is so short, and we ought to give everyone we meet the chance to live the best they can. Mrs. Chester, I know that you're not here, but I need to get all this off my chest. I would have loved you as a mother. I wanted the best for your son always, and so I'd have done anything to make him happy, including living with you no matter how difficult it was. It's sad that you'll never get to experience the love of your grandchildren. Andrea and Andrew are such delightful children and I know that you would have loved them very much. What can I say now but to ask for your forgiveness for going behind your back and marrying your son against your wishes? I also forgive you for all the pain and hurt you caused me. Today I choose to walk away from all the bitterness and anger and let go. I hope you found peace at last."

Harvey was there to receive his wife when she walked into his arms. He held her as she wept silently, letting go of all the hurt and anger that had filled her heart.

"Are you all right?" He asked when he felt that she was calm.

"Thank you for being patient with me," she whispered. "Thank you for waiting for us even when it wasn't easy for you to do so."

"And thank you for coming back to me, my love," Harvey responded. "I feel like a ship that has finally come into the safe harbor."

And with his strong but gentle hands he held Sally close to his heart. Their hearts beat as one, and both of them were home at last.

∽

THANK YOU FOR CHOOSING A PUREREAD BOOK!

We hope you enjoyed the story, and as a way to thank you

for choosing PureRead we'd like to send you this free Western trilogy, and other fun reader rewards…

Click here to claim your free Historical Western trilogy…
https://pureread.com/western

Thanks again for reading.
See you soon!

OTHER BOOKS IN THIS SERIES

If you loved this story why not continue straight away with other books in the series?

Read them all...

Unbroken Promises

Safe in His Western Arms

Dawn at Moonbeam Ranch

Healing the Cowboy's Heart

Winning the Rancher's Heart

OUR GIFT TO YOU

AS A WAY TO SAY THANK YOU WE WOULD LOVE TO SEND YOU THIS BEAUTIFUL TRILOGY FREE OF CHARGE.

Our Reader List is 100% FREE

Click here to claim your free Historical Western trilogy...
https://pureread.com/western

At PureRead we publish books you can trust. Great tales without smut or swearing, but with all of the mystery and romance you expect from a great story.

Be the first to know when we release new books, take part in our fun competitions, and get surprise free books in your inbox by signing up to our Reader list.

As a thank you you'll receive this exclusive Western trilogy - a beautiful collection available only to our subscribers...

Click here to claim your free Historical Western trilogy...

https://pureread.com/western

Made in United States
Troutdale, OR
08/20/2025